nickelodeon
DORA the EXPLORER

Dora's Easter Bunny Adventure

Adapted by Veronica Paz
Based on the teleplay by Rosemary Contreras
Illustrated by Dave Aikins

A Random House PICTUREBACK® Book
Random House New York

randomhouse.com/kids
ISBN: 978-0-449-81442-0
Printed in the United States of America
10 9 8 7 6 5 4 3

It was a beautiful spring day. Dora and Boots were super-excited because it was Easter!

"On Easter we get to dress up in fancy clothes and even wear new hats," Dora said.

"Or you can wear bunny ears like me!" giggled Boots.

They were waiting for a visit from the Hip Hop Bunny. Every year, the Hip Hop Bunny brings all the eggs for their big Easter egg hunt.

The Hip Hop Bunny was on his way to Dora's house with his basket full of eggs, when . . .

. . . that sneaky fox, Swiper, swiped the Hip Hop Bunny's Easter basket and threw it far away!

The Hip Hop Bunny hopped up to Dora and Boots. "*Hola, Dora.* Hi, Boots. I don't know what to say. It's Easter, and that fox took my basket."

"Don't worry, Bunny! We can help you find your basket," said Dora. "Who do we ask for help when we don't know where to go?"

"Map!" shouted Boots.

Map told them that Swiper had thrown the basket far, far away, into the Rainbow River. The basket was floating down the river and was headed toward a waterfall. To get to the Rainbow River, Dora, Boots, and the Hip Hop Bunny had to go through the Flower Garden and past the Petting Farm. But they had to hurry and get the basket before it went over the waterfall!

"Garden, Farm, Rainbow River—got it!" Dora said. *"¡Gracias, Map!"*

"A-tisket, a-tasket! Let's hop in a hurry to get back my Easter basket!" rhymed the Hip Hop Bunny.

"Look, Dora!" exclaimed Boots. "There's the Flower Garden!"

The Hip Hop Bunny started to lead Dora and Boots through the Flower Garden, but some flowers popped up and stood in their way.

"Hmm," Dora said. "We need the flowers to go back down so we can get through the Garden."

"But how can we get them to do that?" asked Boots.

"These flowers speak Spanish," Dora explained. "So to get a flower to go back down, we need to say *'¡Bájate, flor!'*"

Each time they came upon a flower, everyone said *"¡Bájate, flor!"*

And with that, the flowers popped back down to the ground!

"A-tisket, a-tasket! Let's go to the Farm to get back my Easter basket!" rhymed the Hip Hop Bunny.

The trio made it past the Flower Garden and arrived at the Petting Farm—but getting through the Petting Farm was not going to be easy. Their friend Isa explained that they needed to pet all the baby animals first.

"The chicks like to be petted very gently with one finger," said Isa.

Dora and Boots softly petted the chicks with their fingers.

"To get the baby llamas to move, we have to tickle them behind their ears," said Isa. "Let's tickle them together. Tickle, tickle, tickle. . . . Great job!"

Soon the path was clear, and they were able to get past the Petting Farm.

"We made it to the Rainbow River!" cheered Dora. "It's so beautiful! It has all the colors of the rainbow. Let's name them! Red, orange, yellow, green, blue, and violet! Now in Spanish: *rojo, anaranjado, amarillo, verde, azul, y violeta. ¡Muy bien!*"

They saw the Hip Hop Bunny's basket, but it was almost at the edge of the waterfall!

"We need something so we can ride down the river to save the basket," explained Dora. "I think I might have something in my Backpack. Say 'Backpack!'"

"Backpack!" Boots and the Hip Hop Bunny cried.

"What can we use to ride down the river?" asked Backpack. "¡Sí! The giant rubber ducky!"

Dora, Boots, and the Hip Hop Bunny were floating down the river as fast as they could, but the basket was still getting closer to the edge of the waterfall. To help the ducky catch up to the basket, they needed to call out the color of the water that the basket was floating on.

What color did they need to shout? "Blue! *¡Azul!*"

It worked! Dora, Boots, and the Hip Hop Bunny caught up to the basket just before it reached the waterfall's edge!

"My basket filled with eggs! We got it back at last. Now let's get to the party, *rápido*! Let's get there fast!" chanted the Hip Hop Bunny.

Everyone was at Dora's house waiting for the egg hunt to start. They all cheered when they saw Dora, Boots, and the Hip Hop Bunny arrive.

"Yay! *¡Ya llego el conejo!*" cried Tico.

"I'm not a magician, but there's one trick I can do. I can wiggle my nose and ears to make Easter eggs appear for all of you!" exclaimed the Hip Hop Bunny.

Dora invited the Hip Hop Bunny to stay for the Easter party.

"I'm so hip-hop happy! I'm delighted! An Easter party—it's the first time I've been invited!" rhymed the Hip Hop Bunny.

"Come on, Bunny!" exclaimed Dora. "Let's get ready to look for those Easter eggs! *¡Busca los cascarones!*"

Each Easter egg had a special prize inside. Boots found an egg with a toy car, and Dora found an egg with a ring just right for her.

There was just one more egg left to find—a big red one that Dora left just for you! It had a ball inside as a special Easter gift.

Dora and Boots had an *egg*-citing Easter adventure saving the Hip Hop Bunny's basket. And they couldn't have done it without your help! Happy Easter!